PENGUIN POPULAR CLASSICS

THE BOOK OF NONSENSE
AND NONSENSE SONGS

BY EDWARD LEAR

EDWARD LEAR (1812–88). Nineteenth-century artist and writer, best remembered for the absurdist humour of his limericks and nonsense verse.

Edward Lear was born in London in 1812, the youngest son and twentieth child of a stockbroker. He was largely brought up by his elder sister Ann, and worked as a zoological draughtsman until coming under the patronage of the earl of Derby. It was for the earl's grandchildren that he originally wrote *A Book of Nonsense* (1845), a compilation of his own limericks and illustrations. Lear travelled widely, publishing accounts of Italy, Albania and Illyria, Calabria and Corsica. He also visited and produced sketches of Egypt, the Holy Land, Greece and India. His highly inventive verse often had a melancholic undertone, and during his life he suffered from epilepsy and depression. His other collections include *Nonsense Songs, Stories, Botany and Alphabets* (1871), *More Nonsense, Pictures, Rhymes, Botany etc.* (1871) and *Laughable Lyrics* (1877), featuring the Dong and the Pobble who has no toes. Edward Lear died in San Remo in 1888.

This illustrated edition of Lear's verse includes such old favourites as 'The Jumblies' and 'The Owl and the Pussycat', as well as a selection of his limericks.

PENGUIN POPULAR CLASSICS

THE BOOK OF NONSENSE AND NONSENSE SONGS

EDWARD LEAR

PENGUIN BOOKS

PENGUIN BOOKS

Published by the Penguin Group
Penguin Books Ltd, 80 Strand, London WC2R ORL, England
Penguin Putnam Inc., 375 Hudson Street, New York, New York 10014, USA
Penguin Books Australia Ltd, Ringwood, Victoria, Australia
Penguin Books Canada Ltd, 10 Alcorn Avenue, Toronto, Ontario, Canada M4V 3B2
Penguin Books India (P) Ltd, 11 Community Centre, Panchsheel Park,
New Delhi – 110 017, India
Penguin Books (NZ) Ltd, Cnr Rosedale and Airborne Roads, Albany, Auckland,
New Zealand
Penguin Books (South Africa) (Pty) Ltd, 24 Sturdee Avenue, Rosebank 2196, South Africa

Penguin Books Ltd, Registered Offices: 80 Strand, London WC2R ORL, England

www.penguin.com

Selected material in this book was first published in an
Omnibus edition by Frederick Warne & Co. Ltd 1943
Published in Penguin Books 1986
Published in Penguin Popular Classics 1996
6

Printed in Great Britain by Cox & Wyman Ltd, Reading, Berkshire

CONTENTS

THE BOOK OF NONSENSE

Dedication

—

TO THE

GREAT-GRANDCHILDREN,

GRAND-NEPHEWS, AND GRAND-NIECES

OF EDWARD, 13th EARL OF DERBY,

THIS BOOK OF DRAWINGS & VERSES

(The greater part of which were originally made
and composed for their parents)

IS DEDICATED BY

THE AUTHOR

EDWARD LEAR

There was an Old Man with a beard,
Who said, "It is just as I feared!—
    Two Owls and a Hen,
    Four Larks and a Wren,
Have all built their nests in my beard!"

There was a Young Lady of Ryde,
Whose shoe-strings were seldom untied.
    She purchased some clogs,
      And some small spotted dogs,
And frequently walked about Ryde.

There was an Old Man with a nose,
Who said, " If you choose to suppose
    That my nose is too long,
      You are certainly wrong ! "
That remarkable man with a nose.

There was an Old Man on a hill,
Who seldom, if ever, stood still;
    He ran up and down
    In his grandmother's gown,
Which adorned that Old Man on a hill.

There was a Young Lady whose bonnet
Came untied when the birds sat upon it ;
    But she said, " I don't care !
    All the birds in the air
Are welcome to sit on my bonnet ! "

There was a Young Person of Smyrna,
Whose grandmother threatened to burn her ;
    But she seized on the cat,
    And said, " Granny, burn that !
You incongruous old woman of Smyrna ! "

There was an Old Person of Chili,
Whose conduct was painful and silly;
    He sat on the stairs
     Eating apples and pears,
That imprudent Old Person of Chili.

There was an Old Man with a gong,
Who bumped at it all the day long;
    But they called out, "Oh, law!
    You're a horrid old bore!"
So they smashed that Old Man with a gong.

There was an Old Lady of Chertsey,
Who made a remarkable curtsey;
    She twirled round and round
    Till she sank underground,
Which distressed all the people of Chertsey.

There was an Old Man in a tree,
Who was horribly bored by a bee;
 When they said, "Does it buzz?"
 He replied, "Yes, it does!
It's a regular brute of a bee!"

There was an Old Man with a flute.
A " sarpint " ran into his boot ;
    But he played day and night,
    Till the " sarpint " took flight,
And avoided that man with a flute.

There was a Young Lady whose chin
Resembled the point of a pin ;
    So she had it made sharp,
    And purchased a harp,
And played several tunes with her chin.

There was an Old Man of Kilkenny,
Who never had more than a penny;
    He spent all that money
    In onions and honey,
That wayward Old Man of Kilkenny.

There was an Old Person of Ischia,
Whose conduct grew friskier and friskier;
    He danced hornpipes and jigs,
    And ate thousands of figs,
That lively Old Person of Ischia.

There was an Old Man in a boat,
Who said, " I'm afloat ! I'm afloat ! "
    When they said, " No, you ain't ! "
    He was ready to faint,
That unhappy Old Man in a boat.

There was a Young Lady of Portugal,
Whose ideas were excessively nautical;
    She climbed up a tree
    To examine the sea,
But declared she would never leave Portugal.

There was an Old Man of Moldavia,
Who had the most curious behaviour;
    For while he was able
    He slept on a table,
That funny Old Man of Moldavia.

There was an Old Man of Madras,
Who rode on a cream-coloured ass;
    But the length of its ears
    So promoted his fears,
That it killed that Old Man of Madras.

There was an Old Person of Leeds,
Whose head was infested with beads;
    She sat on a stool
    And ate gooseberry-fool,
Which agreed with that Person of Leeds.

There was an Old Person of Hurst,
Who drank when he was not athirst;
    When they said, " You'll grow fatter ! "
    He answered, " What matter ? "
That globular Person of Hurst.

There was a Young Person of Crete,
Whose toilet was far from complete;
    She dressed in a sack
    Spickle-speckled with black,
That ombliferous Person of Crete.

There was an Old Man of the Isles,
Whose face was pervaded with smiles;
   He sung " High dum diddle,"
   And played on the fiddle,
That amiable man of the Isles.

There was an Old Person of Buda,
Whose conduct grew ruder and ruder,
    Till at last with a hammer
    They silenced his clamour,
By smashing that Person of Buda.

There was an Old Man of Columbia,
Who was thirsty and called out for some beer!
 But they brought it quite hot
 In a small copper pot,
Which disgusted that Man of Columbia.

There was a Young Lady of Dorking,
Who bought a large bonnet for walking;
    But its colour and size
    So bedazzled her eyes,
That she very soon went back to Dorking.

There was an Old Man who supposed
That the street door was partially closed;
    But some very large rats
    Ate his coats and his hats,
While that futile Old Gentleman dozed.

There was an Old Man of the West,
Who wore a pale plum-coloured vest;
    When they said, " Does it fit ? "
    He replied, " Not a bit ! "
That uneasy Old Man of the West.

There was an Old Man of the Wrekin,
Whose shoes made a horrible creaking;
    But they said, " Tell us whether
    Your shoes are of leather,
Or of what, you Old Man of the Wrekin? "

There was a Young Lady whose eyes
Were unique as to colour and size;
    When she opened them wide,
    People all turned aside,
And started away in surprise.

There was a Young Lady of Norway,
Who casually sat in a doorway;
    When the door squeezed her flat,
    She exclaimed, " What of that ? "
This courageous Young Lady of Norway.

There was an Old Man of Vienna,
Who lived upon tincture of senna;
    When that did not agree
    He took camomile tea,
That nasty Old Man of Vienna.

There was an Old Person whose habits
Induced him to feed upon rabbits;
    When he'd eaten eighteen
    He turned perfectly green,
Upon which he relinquished those habits.

There was an Old Person of Dover,
Who rushed through a field of blue clover;
    But some very large bees
    Stung his nose and his knees,
So he very soon went back to Dover.

There was an Old Man of Marseilles,
Whose daughters wore bottle-green veils;
    They caught several fish,
    Which they put in a dish,
And sent to their Pa at Marseilles.

There was an Old Person of Cadiz,
Who was always polite to the ladies;
    But in handing his daughter,
    He fell into the water,
Which drowned that Old Person of Cadiz.

There was an Old Person of Basing,
Whose presence of mind was amazing;
   He purchased a steed,
    Which he rode at full speed,
And escaped from the people of Basing.

There was an Old Man of Quebec,—
A beetle ran over his neck;
    But he cried, " With a needle
    I'll slay you, O beadle ! "
That angry Old Man of Quebec.

There was an Old Person of Philæ,
Whose conduct was dubious and wily;
    He rushed up a palm
     When the weather was calm,
And observed all the ruins of Philæ.

There was a Young Lady of Bute,
Who played on a silver-gilt flute ;
    She played several jigs
    To her uncle's white pigs,
That amusing Young Lady of Bute.

There was a Young Lady whose nose
Was so long that it reached to her toes;
    So she hired an old lady,
    Whose conduct was steady,
To carry that wonderful nose.

There was an Old Man of Apulia,
Whose conduct was very peculiar;
    He fed twenty sons
    Upon nothing but buns,
That whimsical Man of Apulia.

There was an Old Man with a poker,
Who painted his face with red ochre;
    When they said, " You're a Guy ! "
    He made no reply,
But knocked them all down with his poker.

There was an Old Person of Prague,
Who was suddenly seized with the plague;
    But they gave him some butter,
    Which caused him to mutter,
And cured that Old Person of Prague.

There was an Old Man of the North,
Who fell into a basin of broth;
    But a laudable cook
    Fished him out with a hook,
Which saved that Old Man of the North.

There was an Old Person of Mold,
Who shrank from sensations of cold;
   So he purchased some muffs,
   Some furs, and some fluffs,
And wrapped himself up from the cold.

There was an Old Man of Nepaul,
From his horse had a terrible fall ;
    But, though split quite in two,
    With some very strong glue
They mended that Man of Nepaul.

There was an Old Man of th' Abruzzi,
So blind that he couldn't his foot see;
    When they said, " That's your toe ! "
    He replied, " Is it so ? "
That doubtful Old Man of th' Abruzzi.

There was an Old Person of Rhodes,
Who strongly objected to toads;
  He paid several cousins
  To catch them by dozens,
That futile Old Person of Rhodes.

There was an Old Man of Peru,
Who watched his wife making a stew;
    But once by mistake,
    In a stove she did bake
That unfortunate Man of Peru.

There was an Old Man of Melrose,
Who walked on the tips of his toes;
    But they said, " It ain't pleasant
    To see you at present,
You stupid Old Man of Melrose."

There was a Young Lady of Lucca,
Whose lovers completely forsook her;
     She ran up a tree,
     And said, "Fiddle-de-dee!"
Which embarrassed the people of Lucca.

There was an Old Man of Bohemia,
Whose daughter was christened Euphemia;
    But one day, to his grief,
    She married a thief,
Which grieved that Old Man of Bohemia.

There was an Old Man of Vesuvius,
Who studied the works of Vitruvius;
    When the flames burnt his book,
    To drinking he took,
That Morbid Old Man of Vesuvius.

There was an Old Man of Cape Horn,
Who wished he had never been born;
    So he sat on a chair,
    Till he died of despair,
That dolorous Man of Cape Horn.

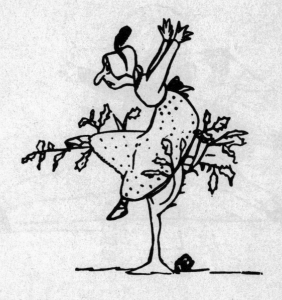

There was an Old Lady whose folly
Induced her to sit in a holly ;
    Whereupon, by a thorn
    Her dress being torn,
She quickly became melancholy.

There was an Old Man of Corfu,
Who never knew what he should do;
So he rushed up and down
Till the sun made him brown,
That bewildered Old Man of Corfu.

There was an Old Man of the South,
Who had an immoderate mouth;
    But in swallowing a dish,
    That was quite full of fish,
He was choked, that Old Man of the South.

There was an Old Man of the Nile,
Who sharpened his nails with a file,
    Till he cut off his thumbs,
        And said calmly, " This comes
Of sharpening one's nails with a file ! "

There was an Old Person of Rheims,
Who was troubled with horrible dreams;
    So, to keep him awake,
    They fed him on cake,
Which amused that Old Person of Rheims.

There was an Old Person of Cromer,
Who stood on one leg to read Homer;
    When he found he grew stiff,
    He jumped over the cliff,
Which concluded that Person of Cromer.

There was an Old Person of Troy,
Whose drink was warm brandy and soy,
    Which he took with a spoon,
    By the light of the moon,
In sight of the city of Troy.

There was an Old Man of the Dee,
Who was sadly annoyed by a flea;
    When he said, " I will scratch it,"
    They gave him a hatchet,
Which grieved that Old Man of the Dee.

There was an Old Man of Dundee,
Who frequented the top of a tree;
    When disturbed by the crows,
    He abruptly arose,
And exclaimed, " I'll return to Dundee."

There was an Old Person of Tring,
Who embellished his nose with a ring;
    He gazed at the moon
    Every evening in June,
That ecstatic Old Person of Tring.

There was an Old Man on some rocks,
Who shut his wife up in a box;
    When she said, "Let me out!"
    He exclaimed, "Without doubt,
You will pass all your life in that box."

There was an Old Man of Coblenz,
The length of whose legs was immense;
    He went with one prance
    From Turkey to France,
That surprising Old Man of Coblenz.

There was an Old Man of Calcutta,
Who perpetually ate bread and butter,
    Till a great bit of muffin,
    On which he was stuffing,
Choked that horrid Old Man of Calcutta.

There was an Old Man in a pew,
Whose waistcoat was spotted with blue ;
    But he tore it in pieces
    To give to his nieces,
That cheerful Old Man in a pew.

There was an Old Man who said, " How
Shall I flee from that horrible cow?
   I will sit on this stile,
   And continue to smile,
Which may soften the heart of that cow."

There was a Young Lady of Hull,
Who was chased by a virulent bull;
    But she seized on a spade,
      And called out, " Who's afraid ? "
Which distracted that virulent bull.

There was an Old Man of Whitehaven,
Who danced a quadrille with a raven;
    But they said, " It's absurd
    To encourage this bird ! "
So they smashed that Old Man of Whitehaven.

There was an Old Man of Leghorn,
The smallest that ever was born;
    But quickly snapped up he
    Was once by a puppy,
Who devoured that Old Man of Leghorn.

There was an Old Man of the Hague,
Whose ideas were excessively vague;
   He built a balloon
    To examine the moon,
That deluded Old Man of the Hague.

There was an Old Man of Jamaica,
Who suddenly married a Quaker;
    But she cried out, " Alack !
    I have married a black ! "
Which distressed that Old Man of Jamaica.

There was an Old Person of Dutton,
Whose head was as small as a button,
    So, to make it look big,
    He purchased a wig,
And rapidly rushed about Dutton.

There was a Young Lady of Tyre,
Who swept the loud chords of a lyre;
    At the sound of each sweep
    She enraptured the deep,
And enchanted the city of Tyre.

There was an Old Man who said, "Hush!
I perceive a young bird in this bush!"
　　When they said, "Is it small?"
　　He replied, "Not at all!
It is four times as big as the bush!"

There was an Old Man of the East,
Who gave all his children a feast;
    But they all ate so much,
    And their conduct was such
That it killed that Old Man of the East.

There was an Old Man of Kamschatka,
Who possessed a remarkably fat cur;
    His gait and his waddle
    Were held as a model
To all the fat dogs in Kamschatka.

There was an Old Man of the coast,
Who placidly sat on a post;
    But when it was cold
    He relinquished his hold
And called for some hot buttered toast.

There was an Old Person of Bangor,
Whose face was distorted with anger!
 He tore off his boots,
 And subsisted on roots,
That irascible Person of Bangor.

There was an Old Man with a beard,
Who sat on a horse when he reared;
    But they said, "Never mind!
    You will fall off behind,
You propitious Old Man with a beard!"

There was an Old Man of the West,
Who never could get any rest;
    So they set him to spin
    On his nose and his chin,
Which cured that Old Man of the West.

There was an Old Person of Anerley,
Whose conduct was strange and unmannerly;
    He rushed down the Strand
    With a pig in each hand,
But returned in the evening to Anerley.

There was a Young Lady of Troy,
Whom several large flies did annoy;
    Some she killed with a thump,
    Some she drowned at the pump,
And some she took with her to Troy.

There was an Old Man of Berlin,
Whose form was uncommonly thin;
    Till he once, by mistake,
    Was mixed up in a cake,
So they baked that Old Man of Berlin.

There was an Old Person of Spain,
Who hated all trouble and pain ;
 So he sat on a chair,
 With his feet in the air,
That umbrageous Old Person of Spain.

There was a Young Lady of Russia,
Who screamed so that no one could hush her;
   Her screams were extreme,—
   No one heard such a scream
As was screamed by that Lady of Russia.

There was an Old Man who said, " Well !
Will *nobody* answer this bell ?
    I have pulled day and night,
     Till my hair has grown white,
But nobody answers this bell ! "

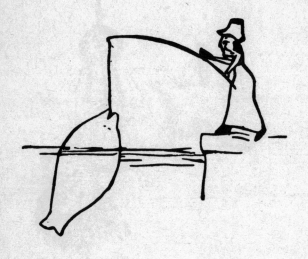

There was a Young Lady of Wales,
Who caught a large fish without scales;
    When she lifted her hook
      She exclaimed, " Only look ! "
That ecstatic Young Lady of Wales.

There was an Old Person of Cheadle,
Who was put in the stocks by the beadle
    For stealing some pigs,
      Some coats, and some wigs,
That horrible Person of Cheadle.

There was a Young Lady of Welling,
Whose praise all the world was a-telling;
    She played on a harp,
    And caught several carp,
That accomplished Young Lady of Welling.

There was an Old Person of Tartary,
Who divided his jugular artery;
    But he screeched to his wife,
    And she said, " Oh, my life!
Your death will be felt by all Tartary!"

There was an Old Person of Chester,
Whom several small children did pester;
    They threw some large stones,
    Which broke most of his bones,
And displeased that Old Person of Chester.

There was an Old Man with an owl,
Who continued to bother and howl;
    He sat on a rail
    And imbibed bitter ale,
Which refreshed that Old Man and his owl.

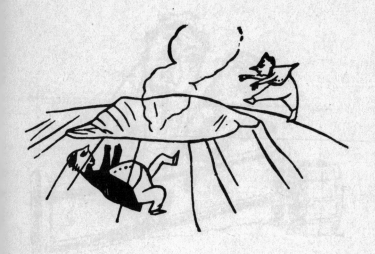

There was an Old Person of Gretna,
Who rushed down the crater of Etna;
    When they said, " Is it hot ? "
    He replied, " No, it's not ! "
That mendacious Old Person of Gretna.

There was a Young Lady of Sweden,
Who went by the slow train to Weedon;
    When they cried, "Weedon Station!"
    She made no observation
But thought she should go back to Sweden.

There was a Young Girl of Majorca,
Whose aunt was a very fast walker;
    She walked seventy miles,
    And leaped fifteen stiles,
Which astonished that Girl of Majorca.

There was an Old Man of the Cape,
Who possessed a large Barbary ape,
　　Till the ape one dark night
　　Set the house all alight,
Which burned that Old Man of the Cape.

There was an Old Lady of Prague,
Whose language was horribly vague;
    When they said, " Are these caps ? "
    She answered, " Perhaps ! "
That oracular Lady of Prague.

There was an Old Person of Sparta,
Who had twenty-five sons and one " darter ";
 He fed them on snails,
  And weighed them in scales,
That wonderful Person of Sparta.

There was an Old Man at a casement,
Who held up his hands in amazement;
    When they said, " Sir, you'll fall ! "
    He replied, " Not at all ! "
That incipient Old Man at a casement.

There was a Young Lady of Clare,
Who was sadly pursued by a bear;
    When she found she was tired,
    She abruptly expired,
That unfortunate Lady of Clare.

There was an Old Person of Ems,
Who casually fell in the Thames;
    And when he was found
      They said he was drowned,
That unlucky Old Person of Ems.

There was an Old Man on whose nose,
Most birds of the air could repose;
    But they all flew away
    At the closing of day,
Which relieved that Old Man and his nose.

There was a Young Lady of Parma,
Whose conduct grew calmer and calmer;
 When they said, "Are you dumb?"
 She merely said, "Hum!"
That provoking Young Lady of Parma.

There was an Old Person of Burton,
Whose answers were rather uncertain ;
    When they said, " How d'ye do ? "
    He replied, " Who are you ? "
That distressing Old Person of Burton.

There was an Old Man of Aosta,
Who possessed a large cow, but he lost her;
    But they said, " Don't you see
    She has rushed up a tree?
You invidious Old Man of Aosta! "

There was an Old Person of Ewell,
Who chiefly subsisted on gruel;
    But to make it more nice
    He inserted some mice,
Which refreshed that Old Person of Ewell.

NONSENSE SONGS

"*I really don't know any author to whom I am half so grateful for my idle self as Edward Lear. I shall put him first of my hundred authors.*"

JOHN RUSKIN.

THE OWL AND THE PUSSY-CAT.

I.

THE Owl and the Pussy-Cat went to sea
  In a beautiful pea-green boat,
  They took some honey, and plenty of
    money,
  Wrapped up in a five-pound note.
The Owl looked up to the stars above,
  And sang to a small guitar,
" O lovely Pussy ! O Pussy, my love,
  " What a beautiful Pussy you are,
      " You are,
      " You are !
" What a beautiful Pussy you are ! "

II.

Pussy said to the Owl, " You elegant fowl !

" How charmingly sweet you sing !

"O let us be married ! too long we have tarried:

" But what shall we do for a ring ? "

They sailed away for a year and a day,

To the land where the Bong-tree grows,

And there in a wood a Piggy-wig stood,

With a ring at the end of his nose,

His nose,

His nose,

With a ring at the end of his nose.

III.

" Dear Pig, are you willing to sell for one shilling

" Your ring ? " Said the Piggy, " I will."

So they took it away, and were married next day
  By the Turkey who lives on the hill.
They dinèd on mince, and slices of quince,[1]
  Which they ate with a runcible spoon;
And hand in hand, on the edge of the sand,
  They danced by the light of the moon,
     The moon,
     The moon,
  They danced by the light of the moon.

[1] Mr. Lear was delighted when I showed to him that this couple were reviving the old law of Solon, that the Athenian bride and bridegroom should eat a quince together at their wedding.—E. S.

THE DUCK AND THE KANGAROO.

I.

S AID the Duck to the Kangaroo,
     " Good gracious ! how you hop !
    " Over the fields and the water too,
   " As if you never would stop !
" My life is a bore in this nasty pond,
" And I long to go out in the world beyond !
    " I wish I could hop like you ! "
    Said the Duck to the Kangaroo.

II.

" Please give me a ride on your back ! '
    Said the Duck to the Kangaroo.
" I would sit quite still, and say nothing but
    ' Quack,'
    " The whole of the long day through !

" And we'd go to the Dee, and the Jelly Bo Lee,

" Over the land, and over the sea ;—

" Please take me a ride ! O do !"

Said the Duck to the Kangaroo.

III.

Said the Kangaroo to the Duck,

" This requires some little reflection ;

" Perhaps on the whole it might bring me luck,

" And there seems but one objection,

" Which is, if you'll let me speak so bold,

" Your feet are unpleasantly wet and cold,

" And would probably give me the roo-

" Matiz !" said the Kangaroo.

IV.

Said the Duck, " As I sate on the rocks,
  " I have thought over that completely,
" And I bought four pairs of worsted socks
  " Which fit my web-feet neatly.
" And to keep out the cold I've bought a cloak,
" And every day a cigar I'll smoke,
  " All to follow my own dear true
  " Love of a Kangaroo ! "

V.

Said the Kangaroo, " I'm ready !
  " All in the moonlight pale ;
" But to balance me well, dear Duck, sit steady !
  " And quite at the end of my tail ! "

So away they went with a hop and a bound,
And they hopped the whole world three times
  round;
  And who so happy,—O who,
  As the Duck and the Kangaroo?

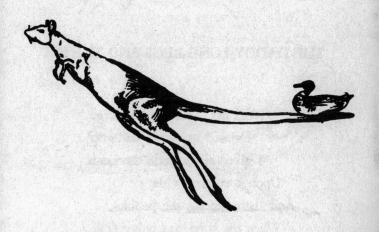

THE DADDY LONG-LEGS AND THE FLY.

I.

ONCE Mr. Daddy Long-Legs,
  Dressed in brown and gray,
  Walked about upon the sands
  Upon a summer's day;
And there among the pebbles,
  When the wind was rather cold,
He met with Mr. Floppy Fly,
  All dressed in blue and gold.
And as it was too soon to dine,
They drank some Periwinkle-wine,

And played an hour two, or more,
At battlecock and shuttledore.

II.

Said Mr. Daddy Long-Legs
  To Mr. Floppy Fly,
" Why do you never come to court?
  " I wish you'd tell me why.
" All gold and shine, in dress so fine,
  " You'd quite delight the court.
" Why do you never go at all?
  " I really think you *ought !*
" And if you went, you'd see such sights !
" Such rugs ! and jugs ! and candle-lights !
" And more than all, the King and Queen,
" One in red, and one in green ! "

III.

" O Mr. Daddy Long-Legs,"
  Said Mr. Floppy Fly,

" It's true I never go to court,
 " And I will tell you why.
" If I had six long legs like yours,
 " At once I'd go to court !
" But oh ! I can't, because *my* legs
 " Are so extremely short.
" And I'm afraid the King and Queen
" (One in red, and one in green)
" Would say aloud, ' You are not fit,
" ' You Fly, to come to court a bit ! '

IV.

" O Mr. Daddy Long-Legs,"
 Said Mr. Floppy Fly,
" I wish you'd sing one little song !
 " One mumbian melody !
" You used to sing so awful well
 " In former days gone by,
" But now you never sing at all ;
 " I wish you'd tell me why :

" For if you would, the silvery sound
" Would please the shrimps and cockles round,
" And all the crabs would gladly come
" To hear you sing, ' Ah, Hum di Hum ! ' "

v.

Said Mr. Daddy Long-Legs,
  " I can never sing again !
" And if you wish, I'll tell you why,
  " Although it gives me pain.
" For years I could not hum a bit,
  " Or sing the smallest song ;
" And this the dreadful reason is,
  " My legs are grown too long !
" My six long legs, all here and there,
" Oppress my bosom with despair ;
" And if I stand, or lie, or sit,
" I cannot sing one single bit ! "

vi.

So Mr. Daddy Long-legs
  And Mr. Floppy Fly

Sat down in silence by the sea,
  And gazed upon the sky.
They said, " This is a dreadful thing !
  " The world has all gone wrong,
" Since one has legs too short by half,
  " The other much too long !
" One never more can go to court,
" Because his legs have grown too short ;
" The other cannot sing a song,
" Because his legs have grown too long ! "

VII.

Then Mr. Daddy Long-legs
  And Mr. Floppy Fly
Rushed downward to the foaming sea
  With one sponge-taneous cry ;
And there they found a little boat
  Whose sails were pink and gray ;
And off they sailed among the waves
  Far, and far away.

They sailed across the silent main
And reached the great Gromboolian plain;
And there they play for evermore
At battlecock and shuttledore.

THE JUMBLIES.

I.

THEY went to sea in a Sieve, they did,
　　In a Sieve they went to sea :
　　In spite of all their friends could say,
On a winter's morn, on a stormy day,
　　In a Sieve they went to sea !
And when the Sieve turned round and round,
And every one cried, "You'll all be drowned !"
They called aloud, "Our Sieve ain't big,
"But we don't care a button ! we don't care a fig !
　　"In a Sieve we'll go to sea !"

Far and few, far and few,
   Are the lands where the Jumblies live;
Their heads are green, and their hands are
   blue,
   And they went to sea in a Sieve.

II.

They sailed away in a Sieve, they did,
  In a Sieve they sailed so fast,
With only a beautiful pea-green veil
Tied with a riband by way of a sail,
  To a small tobacco-pipe mast;
And every one said, who saw them go,
" O won't they be soon upset, you know!
" For the sky is dark, and the voyage is long,
" And happen what may, it's extremely wrong
  " In a Sieve to sail so fast!"
   Far and few, far and few,
     Are the lands where the Jumblies live;
    Their heads are green, and their hands are
     blue,
     And they went to sea in a Sieve.

III.

The water it soon came in, it did,
  The water it soon came in;
So to keep them dry, they wrapped their feet
In a pinky paper all folded neat,
  And they fastened it down with a pin.
And they passed the night in a crockery-jar,
And each of them said, " How wise we are !
" Though the sky be dark, and the voyage be long,
" Yet we never can think we were rash or wrong,
  " While round in our Sieve we spin ! "
    Far and few, far and few,
      Are the lands where the Jumblies live ;
      Their heads are green, and their hands are blue,
      And they went to sea in a Sieve.

IV.

And all night long they sailed away;
  And when the sun went down,
They whistled and warbled a moony song
To the echoing sound of a coppery gong,
  In the shade of the mountains brown.

" O Timballo ! How happy we are,
" When we live in a sieve and a crockery-jar.
" And all night long in the moonlight pale,
" We sail away with a pea-green sail,
  " In the shade of the mountains brown ! "
   Far and few, far and few,
    Are the lands where the Jumblies live ;
    Their heads are green, and their hands are
     blue
    And they went to sea in a Sieve.

v.

They sailed to the Western Sea, they did,
  To a land all covered with trees,
And they bought an Owl, and a useful Cart,
And a pound of Rice, and a Cranberry Tart,
  And a hive of silvery Bees.
And they bought a Pig, and some green Jackdaws,
And a lovely Monkey with lollipop paws,
And forty bottles of Ring-Bo-Ree,
  And no end of Stilton Cheese.

Far and few, far and few,
    Are the lands where the Jumblies live ;
Their heads are green, and their hands are blue,
    And they went to sea in a Sieve.

VI.

And in twenty years they all came back,
  In twenty years or more,
And every one said, " How tall they've grown !
" For they've been to the Lakes, and the Terrible
      Zone,
  " And the hills of the Chankly Bore ; "
And they drank their health, and gave them a feast
Of dumplings made of beautiful yeast ;
And every one said, " If we only live,
" We too will go to sea in a Sieve,—
  " To the hills of the Chankly Bore ! "
    Far and few, far and few,
      Are the lands where the Jumblies live ;
    Their heads are green, and their hands are blue,
      And they went to sea in a Sieve.

THE NUTCRACKERS AND THE
SUGAR-TONGS.

I.

THE Nutcrackers sate by a plate on the table,
  The Sugar-tongs sate by a plate at his
      side ;
And the Nutcrackers said, " Don't you wish we
      were able
  " Along the blue hills and green meadows to
      ride ?
" Must we drag on this stupid existence for ever,
  " So idle and weary so full of remorse,—
" While every one else takes his pleasure and
      never
  " Seems happy unless he is riding a horse ?

II.

" Don't you think we could ride without being
      instructed ?
  " Without any saddle, or bridle, or spur ?
" Our legs are so long, and so aptly constructed,
  " I'm sure that an accident could not occur.

" Let us all of a sudden hop down from the
    table,
   " And hustle downstairs, and each jump on a
     horse !
" Shall we try ? Shall we go ? Do you think we
    are able ? "
   The Sugar-tongs answered distinctly, " Of
     course ! "

III.

So down the long staircase they hopped in a
    minute,
   The Sugar-tongs snapped, and the Crackers
     said " crack ! "
The stable was open, the horses were in it ;
   Each took out a pony, and jumped on his back.
The Cat in a fright scrambled out of the doorway,
   The Mice tumbled out of a bundle of hay,
The brown and white Rats, and the black ones
    from Norway,
   Screamed out, " They are taking the horses
     away ! "

IV.

The whole of the household was filled with
amazement,

The Cups and the Saucers danced madly about,

The Plates and the Dishes looked out of the
casement,

The Saltcellar stood on his head with a shout,

The Spoons with a clatter looked out of the
lattice,

The Mustard-pot climbed up the Gooseberry
Pies,

The Soup-ladle peeped through a heap of Veal
Patties,

And squeaked with a ladle-like scream of
surprise.

V.

The Frying-pan said, " It's an awful delusion ! "

The Tea-kettle hissed and grew black in the
face ;

And they all rushed downstairs in the wildest
confusion,

To see the great Nutcracker-Sugar-tong race.

And out of the stable, with screamings and
   laughter,
   (Their ponies were cream-coloured, speckled
   with brown),
The Nutcrackers first, and the Sugar-tongs after,
   Rode all round the yard, and then all round
   the town.

VI.

They rode through the street, and they rode by
   the station,
   They galloped away to the beautiful shore ;
In silence they rode, and " made no observation,"
   Save this : " We will never go back any
   more ! "
And still you might hear, till they rode out of
   hearing,
   The Sugar-tongs snap, and the Crackers say
   " crack ! "
Till far in the distance, their forms disappearing,
   They faded away.—And they never came back !

CALICO PIE.

I.

CALICO Pie,
    The Little Birds fly
Down to the calico tree,
Their wings were blue,
And they sang "Tilly-loo!"
Till away they flew,—
   And they never came back to me!
    They never came back!
    They never came back!
   They never came back to me!

II.

Calico Jam,
The little Fish swam
Over the syllabub sea,
He took off his hat,
To the Sole and the Sprat,
And the Willeby-wat,—

But he never came back to me!
He never came back!
He never came back!
He never came back to me!

III.

Calico Ban,
The little Mice ran,

To be ready in time for tea,
  Flippity flup,
  They drank it all up,
  And danced in the cup,—
But they never came back to me!
  They never came back!
  They never came back!
They never came back to me!

IV.

  Calico Drum,
  The Grasshoppers come,
The Butterfly, Beetle, and Bee,
  Over the ground,
  Around and round,
  With a hop and a bound,—

But they never came back !
They never came back !
They never came back !
They never came back to me !

MR. AND MRS. SPIKKY SPARROW.

I

ON a little piece of wood,
    Mr. Spikky Sparrow stood;
Mrs. Sparrow sate close by,
A-making of an insect pie,
For her little children five,
In the nest and all alive,
Singing with a cheerful smile
To amuse them all the while,
    Twikky wikky wikky wee,
    Wikky bikky twikky tee.
        Spikky bikky bee!

147

II.

Mrs. Spikky Sparrow said,
" Spikky, Darling ! in my head
" Many thoughts of trouble come,
" Like to flies upon a plum !
" All last night, among the trees,
" I heard you cough, I heard you sneeze ;
" And, thought I, it's come to that
" Because he does not wear a hat !
 " Chippy wippy sikky tee !
 " Bikky wikky tikky mee !
  " Spikky chippy wee !

III.

" Not that you are growing old,
" But the nights are growing cold.
" No one stays out all night long
" Without a hat : I'm sure it's wrong ! "
Mr. Spikky said, " How kind,
" Dear ! you are, to speak your mind !
" All your life I wish you luck !
" You are ! you are ! a lovely duck !

" Witchy witchy witchy wee !
" Twitchy witchy witchy bee !
" Tikky tikky tee !

IV.

" I was also sad, and, thinking,
" When one day I saw you winking,
" And I heard you sniffle-snuffle,
" And I saw your feathers ruffle;
" To myself I sadly said,
" She's neuralgia in her head !
" That dear head has nothing on it !
" Ought she not to wear a bonnet ?
" Witchy kitchy kitchy wee !
" Spikky wikky mikky bee !
" Chippy wippy chee !

V.

" Let us both fly up to town !
" There I'll buy you such a gown !
" Which, completely in the fashion,
" You shall tie a sky-blue sash on.

" And a pair of slippers neat,
" To fit your darling little feet,
" So that you will look and feel
" Quite galloobious and genteel !
    " Jikky wikky bikky see !
      " Chicky bikky wikky bee !
        " Twicky witchy wee ! "

VI.

So they both to London went,
Alighting on the Monument,
Whence they flew down swiftly—pop,
Into Moses' wholesale shop ;
There they bought a hat and bonnet,
And a gown with spots upon it,
A satin sash of Cloxam blue,
And a pair of slippers too.
      Zikky wikky mikky bee !
      Witchy witchy mitchy kee !
        Sikky tikky wee !

VII.

Then when so completely drest,
Back they flew and reached their nest.
Their children cried, "O Ma and Pa!
"How truly beautiful you are!"
Said they, "We trust that cold or pain
"We shall never feel again!
"While, perched on tree, or house, or steeple,
"We now shall look like other people.

    "Witchy witchy witchy wee!
    "Twikky mikky bikky bee!
      "Zikky sikky tee!"

THE BROOM, THE SHOVEL, THE POKER,
AND THE TONGS.

I.

THE Broom and the Shovel, the Poker and
Tongs,
They all took a drive in the Park,
And they each sang a song, Ding-a-dong,
Ding-a-dong,
Before they went back in the dark.

Mr. Poker he sate quite upright in the coach,
　　Mr. Tongs made a clatter and clash,
Miss Shovel was dressed all in black (with a
　　　　brooch),
　　Mrs. Broom was in blue (with a sash).
　　　　Ding-a-dong ! Ding-a-dong !
　　　　And they all sang a song !

　　　　　　II.
" O Shovely so lovely ! " the Poker he sang,
　" You have perfectly conquered my heart !
" Ding-a-dong ! Ding-a-dong ! If you're pleased
　　　with my song
　　" I will feed you with cold apple tart !
" When you scrape up the coals with a delicate
　　　sound,
　　" You enrapture my life with delight !
" Your nose is so shiny ! your head is so round !
　　" And your shape is so slender and bright !
　　　　" Ding-a-dong ! Ding-a-dong !
　　　　" Ain't you pleased with my song ? "

III.

"Alas! Mrs. Broom!" sighed the Tongs in
his song,

"O is it because I'm so thin,

"And my legs are so long—Ding-a-dong!
Ding-a-dong!—

"That you don't care about me a pin?

"Ah! fairest of creatures, when sweeping the
room,

"Ah! why don't you heed my complaint!

"Must you needs be so cruel, you beautiful
Broom,

"Because you are covered with paint?

"Ding-a-dong! Ding-a-dong!

"You are certainly wrong!"

IV.

Mrs. Broom and Miss Shovel together they sang,

"What nonsense you're singing to-day!"

Said the Shovel, "I'll certainly hit you a bang!"

Said the Broom, "And I'll sweep you away!"

So the Coachman drove homeward as fast as he
    could,
 Perceiving their anger with pain ;
But they put on the kettle, and little by little,
 They all became happy again.
   Ding-a-dong ! Ding-a-dong !
   There's an end of my song !

THE TABLE AND THE CHAIR.

I

SAID the Table to the Chair,
    " You can hardly be aware
    " How I suffer from the heat,
" And from chilblains on my feet!
" If we took a little walk,
" We might have a little talk!
" Pray let us take the air!"
Said the Table to the Chair.

II.

Said the Chair unto the Table,
"Now you *know* we are not able!
"How foolishly you talk,
"When you know we *cannot* walk!"
Said the Table with a sigh,
"It can do no harm to try;
"I've as many legs as you,
"Why can't we walk on two?"

III.

So they both went slowly down,
And walked about the town
With a cheerful bumpy sound,
As they toddled round and round.
And everybody cried,
As they hastened to their side,
"See! the Table and the Chair
"Have come out to take the air!"

IV.

But in going down an alley,
To a castle in the valley,
They completely lost their way,
And wandered all the day,
Till, to see them safely back.
They paid a Ducky-quack,
And a Beetle, and a Mouse,
Who took them to their house.

V.

Then they whispered to each other,
" O delightful little brother!
" What a lovely walk we've taken!
" Let us dine on Beans and Bacon!"

So the Ducky and the leetle
Browny-Mousy and the Beetle
Dined, and danced upon their heads
Till they toddled to their beds.

THE DONG WITH A LUMINOUS NOSE.

WHEN awful darkness and silence reign
    Over the great Gromboolian plain,
  Through the long, long wintry nights;—
When the angry breakers roar
As they beat on the rocky shore;—
    When Storm-clouds brood on the towering
        heights
Of the Hills of the Chankly Bore:—

Then, through the vast and gloomy dark,
There moves what seems a fiery spark,
  A lonely spark with silvery rays

Piercing the coal-black night,—
   A meteor strange and bright :—
Hither and thither the vision strays,
   A single lurid light.

Slowly it wanders,—pauses,—creeps,—
Anon it sparkles,—flashes and leaps ;
And ever as onward it gleaming goes
A light on the Bong-tree stems it throws.
And those who watch at that midnight hour
From Hall or Terrace, or lofty Tower,
Cry, as the wild light passes along,—
      " The Dong !—the Dong !
   " The wandering Dong through the forest
         goes !
      " The Dong ! the Dong !
   " The Dong with a luminous Nose ! "

      Long years ago
      The Dong was happy and gay,
Till he fell in love with a Jumbly Girl
Who came to those shores one day.

For the Jumblies came in a Sieve, they did,—
Landing at eve near the Zemmery Fidd
 Where the Oblong Oysters grow,
 And the rocks are smooth and gray.
And all the woods and the valleys rang
With the Chorus they daily and nightly sang,—
 " Far and few, far and few,
  Are the lands where the Jumblies live ;
  Their heads are green, and their hands are blue,
  And they went to sea in a Sieve."

Happily, happily passed those days !
 While the cheerful Jumblies staid ;
 They danced in circlets all night long,
 To the plaintive pipe of the lively Dong,
 In moonlight, shine, or shade.
For day and night he was always there
By the side of the Jumbly Girl so fair,
With her sky-blue hands, and her sea-green hair,
Till the morning came of that hateful day
When the Jumblies sailed in their Sieve away,

And the Dong was left on the cruel shore
Gazing—gazing for evermore,—
Ever keeping his weary eyes on
That pea-green sail on the far horizon,—
Singing the Jumbly Chorus still
As he sate all day on the grassy hill,—

> " *Far and few, far and few,*
> *Are the lands where the Jumblies live ;*
> *Their heads are green, and their hands are blue,*
> *And they went to sea in a Sieve.*"

But when the sun was low in the West,
  The Dong arose and said,—
 " What little sense I once possessed
 " Has quite gone out of my head ! "
And since that day he wanders still
By lake and forest, marsh and hill,
Singing—" O somewhere, in valley or plain
" Might I find my Jumbly Girl again !
" For ever I'll seek by lake and shore
" Till I find my Jumbly Girl once more ! "

Playing a pipe with silvery squeaks,
Since then his Jumbly Girl he seeks,
And because by night he could not see,
He gathered the bark of the Twangum Tree
  On the flowery plain that grows.
  And he wove him a wondrous Nose,—
A Nose as strange as a Nose could be !
Of vast proportions and painted red,
And tied with cords to the back of his head.
  —In a hollow rounded space it ended
  With a luminous lamp within suspended
    All fenced about
    With a bandage stout
    To prevent the wind from blowing it
    out ;—
  And with holes all round to send the light,
  In gleaming rays on the dismal night.

And now each night, and all night long,
Over those plains still roams the Dong ;

And above the wail of the Chimp and Snipe
You may hear the squeak of his plaintive pipe
While ever he seeks, but seeks in vain
To meet with his Jumbly Girl again ;
Lonely and wild—all night he goes,—
The Dong with a luminous Nose !
And all who watch at the midnight hour,
From Hall or Terrace, or lofty Tower,
Cry, as they trace the Meteor bright,
Moving along through the dreary night,—
    " This is the hour when forth he goes,
    " The Dong with a luminous Nose !
    " Yonder—over the plain he goes ;
        " He goes !
        " He goes ;
    " The Dong with a luminous Nose ! "

THE TWO OLD BACHELORS.

TWO old Bachelors were living in one house ;
    One caught a Muffin, the other caught
    a Mouse.

Said he who caught the Muffin to him who
    caught the Mouse,—

" This happens just in time ! For we've nothing
    in the house,

" Save a tiny slice of lemon and a teaspoonful of
    honey,

" And what to do for dinner—since we haven't
    any money ?

" And what can we expect if we haven't any
    dinner,
" But to lose our teeth and eyelashes and keep
    on growing thinner ? "

Said he who caught the Mouse to him who
    caught the Muffin,—
" We might cook this little Mouse, if we only
    had some Stuffin' !
" If we had but Sage and Onion we could do
    extremely well,
" But how to get that Stuffin' it is difficult to
    tell ! "—

Those two old Bachelors ran quickly to the town
And asked for Sage and Onion as they wandered
    up and down ;
They borrowed two large Onions, but no Sage
    was to be found
In the Shops, or in the Market, or in all the
    Gardens round.

But some one said,—" A hill there is, a little to
    the north,

" And to its purpledicular top a narrow way
    leads forth ;—

" And there among the rugged rocks abides an
    ancient Sage,—

" An earnest Man, who reads all day a most
    perplexing page.

" Climb up, and seize him by the toes !—all
    studious as he sits,—

" And pull him down,—and chop him into end-
    less little bits !

" Then mix him with your Onion (cut up likewise
    into Scraps),—

" When your Stuffin' will be ready—and very
    good : perhaps."

Those two old Bachelors without loss of time

The nearly purpledicular crags at once began to
    climb ;

And at the top, among the rocks, all seated in a
    nook,

They saw that Sage, a-reading of a most enormous
    book.

" You earnest Sage ! " aloud they cried, " your
    book you've read enough in !—

" We wish to chop you into bits to mix you into
    Stuffin' ! "

But that old Sage looked calmly up, and with
    his awful book,

At those two Bachelors' bald heads a certain aim
    he took ;—

And over crag and precipice they rolled pro-
    miscuous down,—

At once they rolled, and never stopped in lane
    or field or town,—

And when they reached their house, they found
    (besides their want of Stuffin'),

The Mouse had fled ;—and, previously, had
    eaten up the Muffin.

They left their home in silence by the once
    convivial door,

And from that hour those Bachelors were never
    heard of more.

THE PELICAN CHORUS.

KING and Queen of the Pelicans we;
   No other Birds so grand we see!
None but we have feet like fins!
With lovely leathery throats and chins!
   Ploffskin, Pluffskin, Pelican jee!
   We think no birds so happy as we!
   Plumpskin, Ploshkin, Pelican jill!
   We think so then, and we thought so still!

We live on the Nile. The Nile we love.
By night we sleep on the cliffs above.
By day we fish, and at eve we stand
On long bare islands of yellow sand.
And when the sun sinks slowly down
And the great rock walls grow dark and brown,
Where the purple river rolls fast and dim
And the ivory Ibis starlike skim,
Wing to wing we dance around,—
Stamping our feet with a flumpy sound,—
Opening our mouths as Pelicans ought,
And this is the song we nightly snort:

 Ploffskin, Pluffskin, Pelican jee!
 We think no Birds so happy as we!
 Plumpskin, Ploshkin, Pelican jill!
 We think so then, and we thought so still.

Last year came out our Daughter, Dell;
And all the Birds received her well.
To do her honour, a feast we made
For every bird that can swim or wade.

Herons and Gulls, and Cormorants black,
Cranes, and Flamingoes with scarlet back,
Plovers and Storks, and Geese in clouds,
Swans and Dilberry Ducks in crowds.
Thousands of Birds in wondrous flight!
They ate and drank and danced all night,
And echoing back from the rocks you heard
Multitude-echoes from Bird and Bird,—

 Ploffskin, Pluffskin, Pelican jee!
 We think no Birds so happy as we!
 Plumpskin, Ploshkin, Pelican jill!
 We think so then, and we thought so still!

Yes, they came; and among the rest,
The King of the Cranes all grandly dressed.
Such a lovely tail! Its feathers float
Between the ends of his blue dress-coat;
With pea-green trowsers all so neat,
And a delicate frill to hide his feet,—
(For though no one speaks of it, every one knows,
He has got no webs between his toes!)

As soon as he saw our Daughter Dell,
In violent love that Crane King fell,—
On seeing her waddling form so fair,
With a wreath of shrimps in her short white hair,
And before the end of the next long day,
Our Dell had given her heart away;
For the King of the Cranes had won that heart,
With a Crocodile's egg and a large fish-tart.
She vowed to marry the King of the Cranes,
Leaving the Nile for stranger plains;
And away they flew in a gathering crowd
Of endless birds in a lengthening cloud.
    Ploffskin, Pluffskin, Pelican jee!
    We think no Birds so happy as we!
    Plumpskin, Ploshkin, Pelican jill!
    We think so then, and we thought so still!

And far away in the twilight sky,
We heard them singing a lessening cry,—
Farther and farther till out of sight,
And we stood alone in the silent night!

Often since, in the nights of June,
We sit on the sand and watch the moon ; —
She has gone to the great Gromboolian plain,
And we probably never shall meet again !
Oft, in the long still nights of June,
We sit on the rocks and watch the moon ;—
——She dwells by the streams of the Chankly
      Bore,
And we probably never shall see her more.

    Ploffskin, Pluffskin, Pelican jee !
    We think no Birds so happy as we !
    Plumpskin, Ploshkin, Pelican jill !
    We think so then, and we thought so still !